This book belongs to

_____

Dedication

Don White. My Paw Paw who taught
me that every tree has its place.

Morgan, Wyatt, and Welles

EVERY TREE
HAS
ITS PLACE

written By
Zach Wilson

Illustrated By
Mutiara Arum

The Great Wood was a wonderful place where every tree and animal had a great role in helping each other.

In a snug little home nestled within
The Great Wood, lived Paw Paw Bear
and Grandma Bear.

Their beloved Grandcub, Bridger Bear,
loved visiting them.

Paw Paw Bear had a kind heart.
He loved caring for his garden
and young Bridger.

Bridger Bear, a spirited cub, had a knack for telling jokes and playing games that brought laughter to everyone around him.

One bright morning, while the two were eating breakfast, Paw Paw Bear leaned over to Bridger and said, "today, we're going on an adventure."

Mouth full of food, Bridger asked, "Where are we going, Paw Paw Bear?" Paw Paw Bear replied, "Ah, that's a secret, Bridger."

With breakfast finished, the bears set off. They stopped once they reached a winding path. Bridger's eyes got big. "Paw Paw Bear, is this path safe? It looks a bit scary," said Bridger.

Paw Paw Bear patted Bridger's back
and said, "don't be afraid. I've walked
this path many times before, and I'll
be right here with you."

Bridger looked up expectantly. "will you tell me where we're going?" he asked. Paw Paw Bear chuckled and said, "that's a surprise."

Leaving the path behind, Paw Paw Bear led Bridger toward two trees.

"Are we there yet?" Bridger asked.
Paw Paw Bear smiled and replied,
"Not quite, I want to show you these
two trees. Look closely and tell me
everything you see about them."

Bridger looked at the trees very hard.
At first he didn't see anything special.
They were just two regular trees.

He tried looking harder. He even turned his head upside down to look. His eyes widened with excitement. "Oh, I see it now! One tree has apples, and the other has a bird's nest!" Bridger exclaimed.

"Exactly!" said Paw Paw Bear. "One tree provides food for all, while the other is a home for the bird and its family."

Continuing their journey, Paw Paw Bear and Bridger talked about all the special things they saw along the way.

"Look, Paw Paw!
We're so high up! I
can see the entire
Great Wood!" Bridger exclaimed,
pointing excitedly. "And there's your
house! Maybe if I yell, Grandma Bear
will hear me!"

Taking a deep breath, Bridger
shouted, "GRANDMA BEAR!"
with all his might.

Paw Paw Bear smiled warmly. "This is the highest spot in the whole Great Wood. I brought you here for something important," he said. Bridger's eyes sparkled, "what is it, Paw Paw?" he asked.

In a gentle voice, Paw Paw Bear replied, "Every tree has its place, and so do you."

Bridger scratched his head, "what does that mean?", he asked. Paw Paw Bear explained,

"In the Bible, in the book of Ephesians,

Chapter 2, Verse 10, it says, 'For we are God's handiwork, created in Christ Jesus to do good works, which God prepared in advance for us to do.'"

Paw Paw Bear continued, "Just as God has given each tree unique talents to help others, He has also blessed you and me with special ways to help those around us and do good for Him."

Bridger's face lit up. "so, my jokes can bring smiles to the animals in the Great Wood?" he exclaimed. Paw Paw Bear nodded. "Exactly! God can use your gift of laughter to spread joy to those around you."

"Every tree you see has its place, and so do you. In God's eyes, you are special, created to help others. And in my eyes, you will always be special, my dear Grandcub."

As the sun began to go down, casting a warm golden glow across the Great Wood, Paw Paw Bear and Bridger shared jokes and laughed until their bellies began to grumble.

"I sure hope Grandma bear is cooking something good," said Bridger Bear. Paw Paw Bear Laughed and said, "me too Bridger. Let's go back home."

About the Author

Zach Wilson

Zach Wilson has a deep passion for sharing God's Word with the next generation. He holds an Associate's degree in Christian Ministry from Southeastern University, as well as a Certificate of Ministry from Highlands College specializing in Family and Children's Ministry. Through his children's picture books, Zach hopes to combine his educational background and creative storytelling to lay the foundation of God's Word in young hearts with biblical teachings and values. Zach resides in Lower Alabama, USA, alongside his wife Morgan, their sons Wyatt and Welles, and their dog Lilly. You can find him at zachwilsonbooks. com or @zachwilsonbooks

Mutiara Arum

Mutiara Arum is a talented children's book illustrator from Indonesia. With a passion for creating beautiful illustrations, she has brought to life numerous children's books. Discover her delightful artwork on Amazon or follow her on Instagram @mutiara.arum.7 to see more of her wonderful creations.